THE TERRIBLES ARE TERROR-IFIC!

READ ALL THE BOOKS IN THE SERIES!

Welcome to Stubtoe Elementary

A Witch's Last Resort

Clash of the Gnomes!

WHAT REAL HUMANS AND OTHER CREATURES ARE SAYING ABOUT THE TERRIBLES!

"This book is awesome, dude."

—ETHAN, AGE 8

"It's great! Could use more spiders."

—THEODORE, AGE 7

"ꝯＢDɨo ꙷÊᴧΩ‡•ꙮ Ꙋ̈ËÅ Óᴧᴇ ꝺ̈ŸꙵꙫʚÏ... ꝺꙨÆ Œ̃ Ô̂Å̂Åβ"

—MS. VERNE, PRINCIPAL OF STUBTOE ELEMENTARY

"High-appeal characters presented with plenty of laughs."

—A GROWN-UP (PRESUMABLY) AT *KIRKUS REVIEWS*

THE TERRIBLES

CLASH of the GNOMES!

TRAVIS NICHOLS

RANDOM HOUSE 🏠 NEW YORK

Copyright © 2023 by Travis Nichols

All rights reserved. Published in the United States by Random House
Children's Books, a division of Penguin Random House LLC, New York.

Random House and the colophon are registered trademarks of
Penguin Random House LLC.

Visit us on the Web! rhcbooks.com

Educators and librarians, for a variety of teaching tools,
visit us at RHTeachersLibrarians.com

Library of Congress Cataloging-in-Publication Data
is available upon request.
ISBN 978-0-593-42579-4 (trade)—ISBN 978-0-593-42581-7 (ebook)

The artist used goblin blood and cursed parchment
to create the illustrations for this book.
Interior design by Jen Valero

Printed in the United States of America
10 9 8 7 6 5 4 3 2 1
First Edition

FOR DAISY,

WHO HAS ABSOLUTELY NO INTEREST IN THIS BOOK

CONTENTS

THE FOUNDERS

A PLAY IN ONE ACT, TWO SCENES, IN . . . THREE OR FOUR MINUTES

by CRIMBUS U. TANGLEBONES

CAST OF CHARACTERS

Madame Jethicka Muggy: City planner, first mayor of Creep's Cove. Vampire.

Dr. Shelley: Scientist and inventor. Human.

Celine O: Artist, chef. Harpy.

Chordin: Ship's captain. Gelatinous glob.

Neddie Achooblessyoo: Builder. Undead mummy.

Ms. Verne: Caretaker of Creep's Cove. Eternal omnipotent-ish being (of unmeasurable size or number of tentacles).

Human Townsperson 1: A really mean person.

Human Townsperson 2: Another annoying meddler.

Monster Hunter: Wow, what's their problem?

LOCATION

A torch-lit cave in an undisclosed location and the shore of a smog-covered island way out in the middle of the fish-stinking ocean.

TIME

Oh, some number of years ago.

That's my dad!

ACT I

SCENE I

SETTING: We are deep inside a dark cave. The main light sources are a few scattered torches, a computer screen, and assorted flashing lights from a large machine made of a few consoles, countless wires, and a control panel of levers and buttons.

AT RISE: Madame Jethicka Muggy is sitting at the edge of a small pool fed by dripping stalactites. She is holding

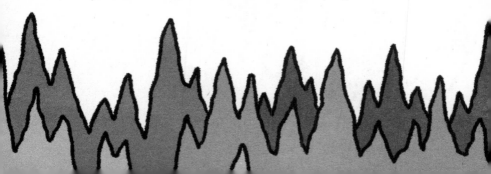

a map and is taking notes on a notepad. Dr. Shelley stands nearby, pulling various levers on a large machine. He is visibly frustrated. Celine O paints at an easel seemingly without a care in the world.

MADAME JETHICKA MUGGY

It's getting worse out there, Dr. Shelley.

(Dr. Shelley slams his hand down on a large button. The machine whirs.)

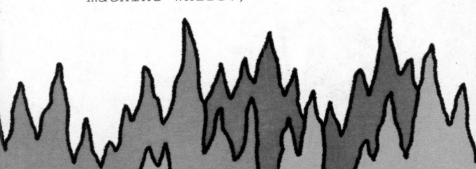

DR. SHELLEY

Indeed. There are seventeen new hunters out there this week, each hungry to make a name for themself.

(ENTER Human Townsperson 1, Human Townsperson 2, and Monster Hunter. Monster Hunter wields a crossbow.)

HUMAN TOWNSPERSON 1
AHA! We found your little lair!

HUMAN TOWNSPERSON 2
We do not LIKE you creatures.

6

HUMAN TOWNSPERSON 1

He speaks for both of us. Dislike!

MONSTER HUNTER

And what do you think you're doing? Planning something?

DR. SHELLEY

That's none of your concern, hunter. And you two. Shame! Shame on you!

HUMAN TOWNSPERSON 2

Ayyy. Shame on *you* for helping this . . . this . . . *monster.*

MADAME JETHICKA MUGGY

Wow, I have a *name.* I am Madame Jethicka Muggy, queen of the night and—

MONSTER HUNTER

We care not for your name! We are here to tell you that your days in polite human society are *over*.

(Monster Hunter fumbles to load his crossbow.)

CELINE O

Okay, so what's about to happen is that we're going to eat every single one of you.

(Madame Jethicka Muggy hisses. Monster Hunter's crossbow bursts into flames. Human Townsperson 1, Human Townsperson 2, and Monster Hunter scream and flee the cave.)

MADAME JETHICKA MUGGY
I can't raise a family in a world like this.

CELINE O

We should have our own place.
Where we can do what we want.

MADAME JETHICKA MUGGY

A place where the pixies and
jackalopes play.

DR. SHELLEY

Yes. Where I can conduct disturbing
and dangerous experiments. And,
Madame, Celine, I believe I have
found just the place. There's
an archipelago of islands way
out . . .

   *(Dr. Shelley points to a map
   on the wall.)*

DR. SHELLEY

This one. Here.

10

MADAME JETHICKA MUGGY

But the sun . . .

DR. SHELLEY

There's a volcano at the center
of the island. With some
modifications, not only can it
supply power to the island, but
it can block out the sun—

MADAME JETHICKA MUGGY

One thousand curses upon it—

DR. SHELLEY

Yes. And it would lock the island
in a permanent haze of dusk. You
could live freely.

CELINE O

It sounds great. Does anyone live
there already?

DR. SHELLEY

There is . . . one resident.
An ancient being with a list
of . . . demands.

MADAME JETHICKA MUGGY

Of course. Whatever they need.
When can we go see this island
for ourselves?

DR. SHELLEY

I've already arranged passage
with a ship's captain friendly to
our cause.

(BLACKOUT)

(END OF SCENE)

ACT I

SCENE 2

SETTING: We see the shore of a smog-covered island. There are a few dead trees, some washed-up seaweed, and assorted debris on the beach. A small, rusty dinghy has recently landed. At stage right is the rocking ocean and an old wooden ship nearby. It is night.

AT RISE: Madame Jethicka Muggy (wearing a large hat and sunglasses), Dr. Shelley, Chordin (wearing a tricorn hat), Celine O, and Neddie Achooblessyou (holding a shovel) stand in the dinghy. They are wearing backpacks and holding camping equipment.

CHORDIN
Friends, welcome to Creep's Cove!

MADAME JETHICKA MUGGY
Thank you, Captain. But . . . are we settled on the name? Perhaps we should workshop it a bit.

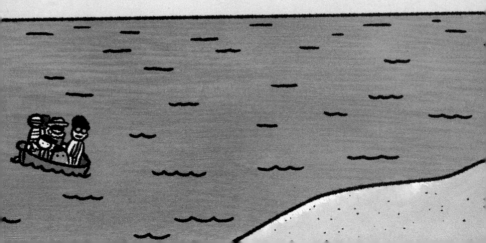

CHORDIN

Sorry, Madame. Celine and I already painted a map. Peach of a name if you ask me.

CELINE O

Chordin is right. I used, like, three different blues on the water. But if you want, I suppose we could—

MADAME JETHICKA MUGGY

Nonono, it's fine. Creep's Cove.
Shall we?

> *(Madame Jethicka Muggy be-*
> *gins to take a step off the*
> *dinghy. Dr. Shelley motions*
> *for her to hold.)*

DR. SHELLEY

Not just yet. Final negotiations.

MADAME JETHICKA MUGGY

Ah, yes yes yes.

> *(Two large tentacles belong-*
> *ing to Ms. Verne enter from*
> *stage left.)*

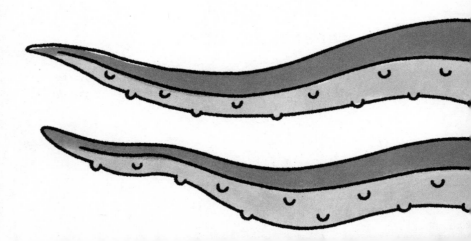

DR. SHELLEY

Ms. Verne, I presume?

MS. VERNE

•Ë¥ſðΣÆÔμΔΩðŒºμiœ£Ü̈qΩ̌ǯ.

(Note: The actor playing Ms. Verne may speak in the gibberish of one's choosing.)

CELINE O

What a beautiful voice! Do you sing any super-sad ballads? I'd love to collab with you.

MS. VERNE

ʒ$ɟ◊μΩ§§ ⊙†βÜ̈Δ$ðÆμ.

MADAME JETHICKA MUGGY

Celine. Later. Certainly, Ms. Verne. Your demands. We have them here.

(Neddie Achooblessyou pulls out a scroll and unfurls it, revealing strange runes written in charcoal.)

DR. SHELLEY
Thank you, Neddie. Ms. Verne, you were given absolute power over your choice of roles in our new society, and you selected *teacher*.

MS. VERNE
Ÿ•Ô$Bʊ°Δ‡.

DR. SHELLEY
Yes. The *only* teacher. As well as principal, school nurse, cafeteria manager, custodian, and

guidance counselor for the entire
school system. I don't see that
being a problem at all.

                NEDDIE ACHOOBLESSYOU
Does anyone else feel like this
might not—
        (Madame Jethicka Muggy shoots
        Neddie Achooblessyou a look
        of anger.)

                NEDDIE ACHOOBLESSYOU
Ooooooooookay.

            MADAME JETHICKA MUGGY
Our spawn will be in good hands,
er, *tentacles* under your care,
Ms. Verne. Thank you.

                    CELINE O
Thank you, Ms. Verne.

(Ms. Verne's tentacles WAVE AND SLITHER offstage. The crew steps out of the dinghy and onto the beach.)

MADAME JETHICKA MUGGY
Now. We must bond together with monsters and monster-adjacent beings from all walks, flights, and slithers of life and afterlife.

CELINE
Beasts of myth and magic.

NEDDIE ACHOOBLESSYOU
The dead and undead.

CHORDIN

Visitors from other worlds.

DR. SHELLEY

Practitioners of forbidden arts
and sciences. And all castaways
from the world of humans.

NEDDIE ACHOOBLESSYOU

One *million* curses upon them. No
offense, Dr. Shelley.

DR. SHELLEY

No, I get it.

MADAME JETHICKA MUGGY
(to the audience)
We welcome you all to gather,
join, and build with us.

CHORDIN/DR. SHELLEY/
NEDDIE ACHOOBLESSYOU/CELINE O
Welcome . . . to Creep's Cove.

MADAME JETHICKA MUGGY
We *sure* about the name, though?

DR. SHELLEY
Let's get started.
(Neddie thrusts their shovel
into the sand.)

(BLACKOUT)

(CURTAIN)

DEAR ELISE,

I hope all is well in Belgium. Things are pretty normal since you've been away. Gilly brought some wiggly swamp sludge to show-and-tell, and it turned out to contain a parasite that engulfed the entire cafeteria, but Ms. Verne quickly turned it into a pretty good stew.

Hi Elise. Vlad here. I've been thinking about getting my band back together. What do you think about running lights and ~~piro pyer~~ pyrotechnics? We'll probably get a record deal soon.

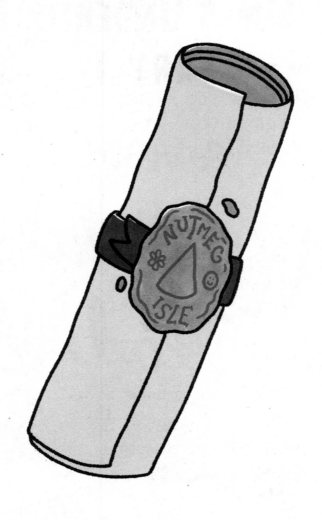

GNOMES UNDERFOOT, PART 1

A goose landed between Quade and Lizzie on the playground at recess, scattering their T.U.F.F. Squad™ Baddleboos game in all directions.

"Oh noooooo," Lizzie wailed. "Let's call it a tie, I guess."

Quade looked around at the array of cards. "But I was winning eighteen to zero."

"I was rounding the corner to a massive comeback," said Lizzie.

"Okay," sighed Quade. "So . . . what's with the goose?"

The goose reached into its basket and pulled out a tiny scroll secured with a red ribbon.

Quade popped the wax seal, unwrapped the ribbon, and uncurled the parchment. The rest of the class gathered around, and Quade read the scroll.

Dear Older-ish Class of Stubtoe Elementary,

A group of us gnomes at Longleaf Primary on Nutmeg Isle have been learning about your island's favorite sport, creepoball. We think it's a fascinating game, and we'd love to test our new skills against yours in a friendly match. We'd be happy to meet you in two weeks' time at your playground. Please send your response back with Strudel.

Your friends,
Basil & the Redcaps
Creepoball's first all-gnome team

△ YES

△ NO

"What be a strudel?" asked Gilly.

"It's a pastry filled with sweet filling," blurfed Bobby. "Apples or peaches or—"

"They want us to **BAKE** for them?" snarled Lizzie. "The nerve of these kids."

The goose cleared her throat and pointed down at her feet. Her talons were painted bright pink with blue letters. S-T-RU-D-E-L.

"Nice to meet you, Strudel," said Frankie.

Quade looked around at his friends. They all nodded. Gilly reached into Strudel's basket, pulled out a little ink bottle and quill, and held it out to Quade. Quade dipped the quill in the ink and checked YES on the parchment.

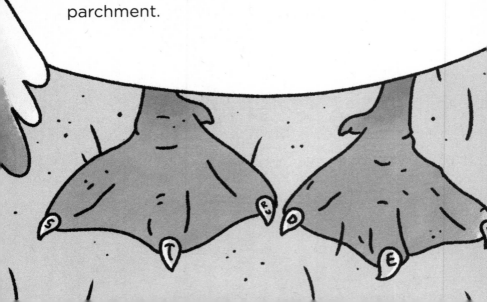

The class was jittery for the rest of the day. They wiggled through Dead Languages, squirmed through Weird Math, and twitched through Ancient Curses. Finally, Ms. Verne rang the end-of-day bell, and everyone rushed up to the front of the classroom and circled Quade.

"Your family is from a gnome-y part of the world. Tell us *everything* about them," demanded Vlad.

"I don't know much," said Quade. "Only what my parents have told me over the years."

Frankie handed Quade a piece of chalk. "We're ready to learn."

Interests: farming, building stuff, animals...

Traits: clever, kind, reclusive, sometimes ~~mischeevi mischu mischieev~~ tricky

Lifespan : 400 years

Then they
return to nature.

Habitat: houses in trees, small cottages, dug out underground, or in caves

Found all over the world

A bunch of them moved to Nutmeg Isle (the next island over) a while back.

(Mostly keep to themselves)

"Let me see if I understand all of this," said Lizzie. "A group of teeny-tiny little kids in silly hats want to play against **US** in a game that **OUR** people invented?" Lizzie fell over laughing.

"This is going to be great!" declared Lobo, imagining a day when he wouldn't be the littlest kid around.

"Side note," said Griff. "I'm going to see if I can find some strufel. It sounds really good."

"Strudel," said Frankie.

"Oh, right," said Griff. "Strudel."

"No—*Strudel*."

Frankie pointed out the window. Everyone turned and saw Strudel squawking at a giant grinning bat.

"Oh no," said Quade. "Should we—"

But the goose and the bat began to dance.

THE EXTREME CLUB

Lizzie and Emma were relaxing in the park against a weedy hill and picking out shapes in the smog.

"That dollop looks like an old tire," said Lizzie.

"WOLLLLFFF," groaned Emma.

"That blob is fully a big old bean," declared Lizzie.

"SCIIIIIISSSSSSOOOORRRRRS," moaned Emma.

"That smeary blotch looks like—"

"HEADS UP!" shouted a voice from behind them.

A cafeteria tray came whooshing down the hill and stopped at Lizzie's and Emma's feet. The tray popped up and hung in the air. What Lizzie and Emma didn't see was Griff, their invisible classmate, holding it.

"Did you *see* that?" asked Griff.

"Of course we didn't," grumbled Lizzie.

"Oh yeah," sighed Griff. "Well, I slid all

the way down that hill. It was—dare I say—*extreme.*"

"Yeah . . . ," muttered Lizzie, rolling her eyes. "Wow. So epic."

Griff stood up a little taller. Nobody saw. "Thanks. Yeah, I like doing extreme things."

"EXTREEEEEEME," groaned Emma.

Lizzie smiled slyly. "You know what's more extreme than a kid sliding down a hill on a cafeteria tray?"

"Tell me and I'll do it," replied Griff.[*]

"*Two* kids sliding down a hill on a cafeteria tray."

"LET'S DOOO THIS!" yelled Griff, clapping Lizzie on the back.

"Oh, not me," said Lizzie, her words oozing with sarcasm. "I'm not neeearly extreme enough."

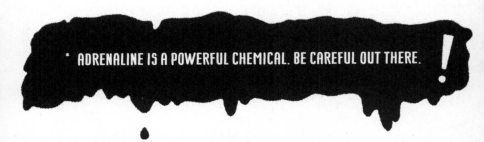

* ADRENALINE IS A POWERFUL CHEMICAL. BE CAREFUL OUT THERE.

"LET'S DOOO THIS!" yelled Griff, clapping Emma on the back.

Emma's arm fell off. "EXTREEEME."

Griff and Emma slid down, down, down, faster and faster, rushing straight for the open front door of Pointy Steffanie's Museum of Loose Thumbtacks.[*]

"TOO EXTREME! TOO EXTREME!" yelled Griff. "Brace for thousands of tiny impacts! This is it! This is—"

BLORF. Everything was silent, sticky, and pink. Griff and Emma had crashed directly into the gelatinous globbiness of

---

* TO GIVE YOU A BETTER GRASP OF THE SITUATION, KNOW THAT IT WAS SATURDAY, WHICH—YEP—IS WHEN FRESH BATCHES OF LOOSE THUMBTACKS ARE DELIVERED TO THE LOBBY OF POINTY STEFFANIE'S MUSEUM OF LOOSE THUMBTACKS.

their friend Bobby as he glorped out of the museum.

Bobby flurbed Griff and Emma out of his glob.

"Whoa," said Griff, counting his fingers and toes. "This has been an excellent first adventure for the Extreme Club."

Bobby flurbled. "What's the Extreme Club? I'm in."

In just over an hour, the Extreme Club had a team charter.[*] It took only a few minutes to type everything on Griff's computer. The bulk of the time was spent looking for the perfect—the most extreme—font to use.

---

[*] A CHARTER IS A DOCUMENT THAT A GROUP DECIDES TO LIVE OR OPERATE BY. IT CAN INCLUDE A GROUP'S PURPOSE, GOALS, RESPONSIBILITIES, THEME SONG LYRICS, MEMBERS, ETC. YOUR CHARTER, YOUR RULES.

43

WE ARE
THE EXTREME CLUB.

WE SEEK THE INTENSE. THE FIERCE. THE MAX.

AT A FORK IN THE ROAD, WE MAKE A NEW PATH.

FIND US AT THE HIGHEST PEAKS AND IN THE DARKEST PITS.

WE ARE EXTREME.

TRULY,
GRIFF! EMMA! BOBBY!

The Extreme Club was out on the prowl. "Okay. I have an idea for our next feat," zorfed Bobby.

"FEEEEEEEEEET," groaned Emma.

"What's your idea?" asked Griff. "I'm in."

"Well," blorfed Bobby. "We're here."

Griff and Emma looked up at the sign where they stood. ANDREW'S CANDIES. "This . . . is a candy store, chumarino," said Griff. "That doesn't . . . feel like an extreme location."

"Juuuuust you wait."

"Welcome to Andrew's Candies!" called a voice from inside. "Enter!"

The Extreme Club stepped/glorped inside and looked around. Each wall was covered in shelves and jars and cabinets full of all sizes and colors and shapes of candies. A row of barrels with scoops lined the far wall, and the labels read things like JELLY BEANS and SMELLY BEANS and YELLY BEANS. At the end of the row was a counter, and behind it was a loose-skinned zombie wearing a frilly suit and a beret.

"We're here for the sour stuff, Andy," flurbed Bobby.

"The name is Andrew, child," said Andrew, pointing at a small sign behind him. "As in Andrew's Candies."

"I'm sorry," ploffed Bobby. "I always think it's called Andy's Candies."

"Well, it absolutely isn't," said Andrew.

"RHYYYMES, THOUUUGGHH," groaned Emma.

"That matters little. I might as well call it *Phyllis's Candies* or *Jasper's Candies* or *Chordin's Candies*. Andrew is my name—therefore—Andrew's Candies."

"Folks really remember rhyming names, though," offered Griff.

Andrew sighed so hard that his loose cheek skin flapped. "Can I help you children with something?"

"Ah, yes," gliffed Bobby. We'd like three Towers of Sours."

"RHYYYYMES," moaned Emma.

"Indeed," said Andrew. He dipped behind the counter and stood back up with three triangular boxes made of yellow cardboard. Each box had seven little doors, numbered one through six. The seventh was taped over.

"The Tower of Sour. Six candies in increasing levels of face-puckering sourness. Not for the faint of tongue."

"Did you say six candies?" asked Griff. "But there are seven doors."

"Yes, that's a misprint, I'm afraid. Yes, that's it. A misprint." Andrew looked around the room nervously.

"Waaaait a second.

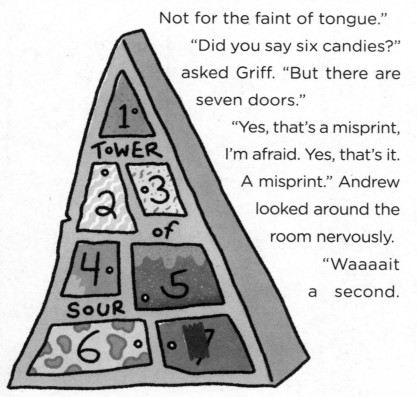

What's the real scoop, candy man?" horfed Bobby.

"Fine." Andrew sighed. "If you must know, when designing the Tower of Sour, I . . . I took things too far. I created a candy with a level of sourness that was just far too extreme. In fact, it—"

"Did you say *extreme*?" asked Griff. "Maybe we forgot to tell you who we are. We're the Extreme Club, and we say we can handle it."

"I don't know," said Andrew, wringing his rotten hands. "At least try the other levels first."

Griff, Bobby, and Emma reached for their boxes and each opened door number six. The candy inside was neon green and covered in some sort of powder. They looked at each other and plopped the candies into their mouths.

Griff shrieked.

Emma's eyes popped out.

Bobby florbled.

The kids flailed around and grabbed at their faces. Andrew produced three small glasses of brown liquid. Without hesitating or asking, the kids grabbed the glasses and chugged the contents. *Aaaahhhhh.*

"A little chocolate seahorse milk usually does the trick," said Andrew. "Now. I suppose we all agree that six levels of sour was more than enough."

Griff and Emma nodded.

"Nope," fliffed Bobby, his tongue bleefling. *"We are the Ethtreme Clubth. We*

theek the intenth. The fierth. The maxth. I'm ready for level theven."

"I have an assortment of other candies you might find *quite* extreme. My Extra-Frothy Root Beer Choosy-Chews are—"

Bobby leebled against the counter. *"I'm ready for level theven."*

"If . . . you say so."

Andrew reached into his collar and pulled out a small key on a silver chain. Then he reached under the counter and pressed a hidden button. A panel on the wall behind him slid open, revealing a small door. Andrew unlocked the door with the key and opened it. Inside was a tiny cubby containing a velvet bag secured with gold rope.

This is really elaborate, thought Griff.

Andrew placed the velvet bag on the counter and untied the rope. He reached in and pulled out a small combination lockbox.

Okay, this is a lot, thought Griff.

Andrew leaned in toward the lock, then gestured for the kids to look away. When their backs were turned, he spun the tiny dials and pressed the latch. It released with a click.

"Okay, children."

Griff, Bobby, and Emma turned back to the counter. Inside the open lockbox was a bright blue nugget with green spots.

"Level seven. The sourest candy ever created, may the Ancient Ones have mercy on my bones."

"EXTREEEEEEEEEME," croaked Emma.

"Now, child, I warn you one last time. You really mustn't—"

Bobby had already jabbled and glorfed the candy.

Bobby's lips hurkled, then hurkled some more. It felt like Bobby's entire Bobbiness was hurkling in on itself. Everything went dark. Then bright again.

Bobby stood up on his feet and looked around. Wait. His what? Bobby looked down. Feet. Legs. Hands. Clothes. What was going on? He looked over and saw a blond vampire behind the counter. She was holding out a hexagon-shaped box made of purple cardboard.

"So as I was saying, Robert, the Suite of Sweet is six candies in increasing levels of

53

sweetness. It's the Mandy's Candies spe-cialty, and I've got one for each of you."

Bobby turned and saw Lizzie and Frankie next to him.

"When did you two get here?"

"We came to this absurd little shop with you, you old dingo," grumbled Frankie.

"Robert, are you feeling okay?" asked Lizzie. "You look a little frazzled. Mandy, do you have a chair?"

The shopkeeper rushed over with a chair and helped Bobby sit down. He woozily looked up at the smiling vampire.

She offered Bobby a damp cloth. "Actually," she said, "my name is Amanda."

"Amanda? I thought this was Mandy's Candies."

"Oh, that." Amanda blushed. "I just thought it would be nicer if it rhymed."

"It doesn't make any sense, though," grumbled Frankie. "Like, who is Mandy?"

Lizzie looked down at her watch. "Oh, I'm afraid our parents will worry if we don't get home soon. We mustn't delay. Robert, are you feeling any better?"

Bobby grabbed Lizzie's forearm and looked at her wrist. The

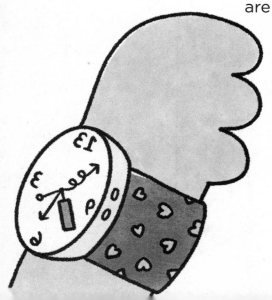

numbers on the watch went up *counter-clockwise.*

"Frankie . . . you're a scientist, right?"

"Dude," groaned Frankie. "We've known each other forever. Yeah. I do science."

Bobby spoke slowly. "Okay, hear me out. Is it possible, scientifically speaking, that someone could do something to such an extreme extent that they somehow—"

Frankie clasped her hand over Bobby's mouth. "That they collapse in on themselves and travel to some sort of nether-dimension? Of course it is."

"Thought so. Amanda?"

"Yes, Robert?"

"I'm going to need the absolute sweetest candy possible. Level *seven.*"

"How . . . how did you know about level seven?"

When Bobby bliffed back into his home dimension, he knocked over a display case of Liquid Larvae Slurpos, breaking several bottles. Griff and Emma rushed to his side.

"Where did you *go*?" shouted Griff.

"It's a long story," wurfled Bobby. "But I think we need to rethink some of the Extreme Team's values."

"SOOOOUUUUUUR," moaned Emma.

"Yeah," agreed Griff. "Sometimes level three is plenty. Four, even."

Griff turned to Andrew. "So . . . we broke some stuff over here."

"Well, considering our . . . transdimensional mishap," offered Andrew, "how about we call it even? No harm done, right?"

Emma and Griff looked at Bobby, then at the broken bottles, then back at Andrew. They shrugged.

"And how about some Extra-Frothy Root Beer Choosy-Chews on the house?" Andrew handed Emma a box of candy. "We're good?"

"GOOOOOD."

As they were headed for the front door to leave Andrew's Candy, a stack of mail plopped through the mail slot. Griff picked it up and carried it over to the counter.

"Wait," said Griff. "Your last name is *Tandy*?"

"Yes. What of it?"

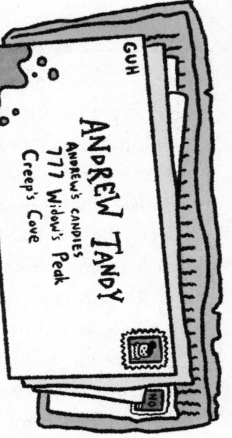

ANDREW TANDY
ANDREW'S CANDIES
777 Widow's Peak
Creep's Cove

ANDREW TANDY
777 WIDOW'S PEAK
CREEP'S COVE

FIFTH NOTICE

Dear Frankie (and Vlad),

Yep! Being back in Belgium is pretty good, but I miss you all. At school, we're learning about the dino-people who live underground and in Dino Ridge. Did you know they were the first to invent the camera, the zipper, and the pizza roll? Vlad, put me down as a "maybe" on lights and pyro stuff. Could be fun, but I have a few other promising offers to sort through.

I hope I can come back soon.

♥Elise

P.S. Frankie, I picked a few different types of moss from around my house. I'm also including a strange bone I found under a pile of rocks. I checked it for curses. Nothing major.

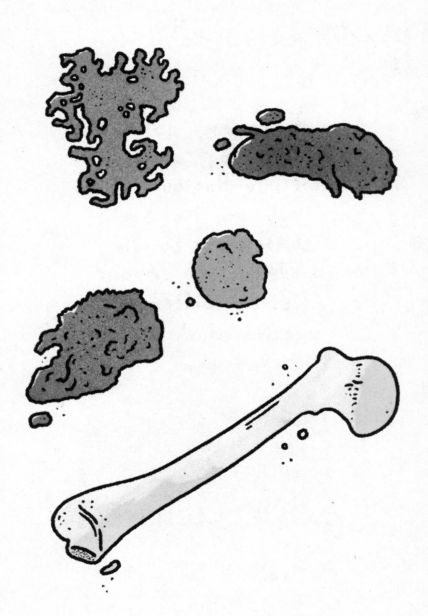

Astronomy got me into geology, which got me into dinosaurs. Then bugs—and that sorta shifted into building models. Then *thaaat* weirdly shifted into puzzles, which led to—

TERRIBLE TOPICS:

TELL US ABOUT YOUR

HOBBIES

My dad and I are fixing up an old sailboat.

I mostly just fetch tools.

64

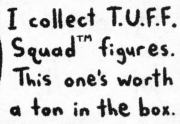

I collect T.U.F.F. Squad™ figures. This one's worth a ton in the box.

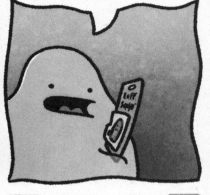

What, so I'm just supposed to *look* at it?

I burn through a new hobby every week.

Is hobby collecting a hobby?

I fight the endless fight.

Against my to-be-read pile. Verily.

A "hobby" is something done in one's spare time for fun.

My music is PAIN.

I curate experiences.

No further questions.

You know what?

RETURN OF
THE MAGGOTS

Griff and Vlad were drawing in the craft corner during free time. Griff was drawing a sword with miniature swords coming out of the handle.

"See, it's like the *sword* has swords," said Griff. "What are you drawing?"

Vlad spun his sheet of paper around so Griff could see. It was a picture of Vlad eating a lollipop in front of a group of people.

"Why are you eating a lollipop?"

asked Griff. "Don't you only, you know, drink, *you know,* blood?"

"That's a microphone," said Vlad. "I'm singing."

"Ohhhh," said Griff. "That's *palpable.*[*] Didn't you have a band?"

"Feels like a thousand years ago," sighed Vlad. "But it was one of the greatest times I can recall."

Griff stroked his chin in that thinky way.[†] "Hmmm. You should play my birthday party at the bowling alley. There's a stage."

Vlad turned into three bats, two rats, and a crow and rushed across the room.

"THE FANS HAVE SPOKEN," announced

---

* GRIFF'S LATEST CATCHPHRASE ATTEMPT. WILL IT CATCH ON?
† NOBODY SAW.

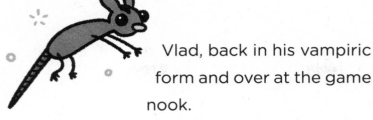

Vlad, back in his vampiric form and over at the game nook.

Erik and Allie didn't look up from their game of "How DARE You Ask Me That?!"*

"Fans?" asked Erik. "Of what? Oh—How DARE you ask me That?!"

Allie took a card from the pile in the middle of the table.

---

* INSTRUCTIONS FOR PLAYING "HOW DARE YOU ASK ME THAT?!" CAN BE FOUND AT THE END OF THIS BOOK.

Vlad snatched the cards out of Erik's and Allie's hands and threw them over his shoulder.

"It's time for a Vlad and the Maggots reunion. Our fans are demanding it."

Allie blinked her gigantic eyes. "Begin. Transmission . . . This.Being.Did.Not.Know. That.Our.Music.Collective.Had.Fans . . . End. Transmission."

"They're demanding it?" asked Erik.

Vlad grabbed Erik by the shoulders. "It's all anyone can talk about."

"Wow . . . ," whispered Erik. He stared

out the window for a few seconds, then cleared his throat. "But it can't be like *last time.*"

The *last time* Erik was referring to was the first and only time their band got together to practice a few months earlier. It started with terrible costumes, continued with feedback on Erik's lyrics that Erik did *not* ask for, and ended with a large explosion and a small fire.

"We've all grown *so* much since then," said Vlad.

Erik looked across the table at Allie. "Vlad and the Maggots forever?"

Allie nodded. "Begin.Transmission . . . Vlad.And.The.Maggots.Forever . . . End. Transmission."

Erik, Vlad, and Allie were rushing to Erik's house after school, when Vlad suddenly grabbed the doorknob of a shop. "Quick stop first."

"Lotsa Heaps? Why do you want to go here?" asked Erik.

Allie peeked through the front window of the thrift store. "Begin.Transmission . . . Perhaps.The.Being.Designated.Vlad.Seeks. New.Costuming.For.Our.Musical.Collective . . . End.Transmission."

Erik took a step back. "Nope. No costumes. No way."

"No costumes," agreed Vlad.

Erik sighed in relief.

Vlad opened the door. "What we need is merch."

Erik and Allie stepped inside and looked around. "Merch?"

Vlad walked a circle around a heap of wet books. "Merch. Merchandise. Swag. T-shirts, hats, stickers. We can turn our fans into walking billboards."

Erik paused. "Maybe we should write a song?"

"Trust the process, Erik," said Vlad. "Follow me."

Vlad, Erik, and Allie wandered about

Lotsa Heaps. They passed piles of old sweatpants, jumbles of broken lamps, stacks of tires, and bundles of rusty tools. Vlad paused by a mountain of kitchenware.

"How much money do you have?"

The Maggots pooled their cash. A few crystals, two copper coins, and a colorful piece of paper with big 5s and a bunch of writing and pictures on it, including the word *Canada.*

"Perfect!" Vlad grabbed a damp cardboard box of assorted wooden spoons and headed toward the register. "*Now* we can go practice."

After about a half hour of noodling around in Erik's garage, Erik and Allie had written a couple of riffs (Erik on his keyboard, Allie on her Sonic Explodinator turned waaay down) and pieced them together into a song. Vlad sat on the floor the whole time writing **VLAD & THE MAGGOTS** on the wooden spoons with a red marker.

Erik looked over at Vlad. "What do you think?"

Vlad looked up from his very important work. "What? Yeah, it's great."

"Begin.Transmission…Initiate.Query.Mode. Does.The.Being.Designated.Vlad.Possess. Lyrical.Notions.Exit.Query. Mode . . . End.Transmission."

Vlad held up a couple of spoons. "Check it out. Twenty-seven official Vlad and the Maggots wooden spoons."

Erik sighed. "Yeah, again, I've never heard of a band having official wooden spoons."

"Exactly," said Vlad. "Oh. Lyric ideas. Write this down."

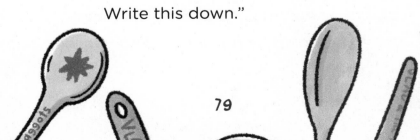

A SPOONFUL OF MAGGOTS.
A SPOONFUL OF MAGIC.
A WORLD WITHOUT MAGGOTS
IS A WORLD WAY TOO TRAGIC.

Vlad dumped the spoons back into the cardboard box and stood up. "Okay, I need to get home for dinner, but let's meet up a few minutes before the show."

"The *show*?"

"Yeah," said Vlad. "Griff's party. I'm sure I told you."

"Griff's party *tomorrow*?!"

"Did I really not mention any of this?"

The next day, Erik and Allie waited in front of the bowling alley. Kids filed in one, two, and three at a time. They waited some more. They could hear bowling pins crashing and laughter coming from inside. They waited some more.

Finally, Vlad strolled up wearing ridiculously huge sunglasses and carrying a pearl-handled walking stick.

"Shall we?"

Allie scoffed. "Begin.Transmission...The.Being. Designated.Vlad. Told.The.Beings. Designated.Allie. And.Erik.To.Meet.Him.In.Front.Of.The.Designated.Location . . . End.Transmission."

"Yeah," said Erik. "We could have been bowling and eating snacks this whole time."

"Sorry, team," said Vlad. "Just wanted us to have a united front. And it took me a while to get *this* perfect."

Vlad whipped off his sunglasses.

"What, eye makeup?" asked Erik. "Neat. Can we go inside now?"

"Rock and roll," declared Vlad.

Vlad and the Maggots strolled in to the bowling alley. Kids were running around, pounding nachos in their faces, and clustering around a small stage where a magician was pulling a rabbit out of a hat, then a small hat out of the rabbit, then a tiny rabbit out of the small hat.

"You the band?" boomed a griffin behind the shoe counter.

Vlad pointed at his eye shadow. "That obvious?"

The griffin pointed at Erik's keyboard.

"Ah."

"You're on after the magician. You've got a thirty-minute set."

Erik's and Allie's jaws dropped. Vlad smiled and pushed them toward the side of the stage.

"We have ONE song," whisper-shrieked Erik. "And it's THREE MINUTES long."

"Okay . . . so we'll improvise," said Vlad. "No problem. Little crowd work, little noodling around on the instruments. We've got this."

"Just play the song ten times," said Erik.

"Begin.Transmission.Let.Us.Play.The.Song. At.One.Tenth.Speed.End.Transmission."

The magician took a deep bow and swept his impossible array of ever-tinier rabbits and hats into a large trunk and carried it offstage.

"You're on!" boomed the manager.

Vlad and the Maggots stepped up onto the stage. Undecided.

Vlad beamed at the crowd. "Two-three-four—"

Erik began playing the opening riff to "A Spoonful of Maggots." Allie played one incredibly long note. Vlad walked back and forth onstage, smiling.

A SPOONFUL OF MAGGOTS.
A SPOONFUL OF MAGIC.
A WORLD WITHOUT MAGGOTS
IS A WOOOORLD . . .
WAAAAAAY!
TOOOOOO!
TRAAAAAAGIC!

Erik finished the song and started again. Allie played a few more incredibly long notes. Vlad sang, *"A SPOOOOOOOOOOOOON."* The crowd began swaying.

During Erik's fifth run-through of the song (and Allie's halfway point), Vlad pulled a crumpled piece of paper from his pocket. It was his book report from a few days before. He sang it. The crowd was going completely wild.

Suddenly, Allie stopped playing and gestured to the others. "Begin.Transmission . . . Our.Alloted.Time.Has.Elapsed.This.Concludes. Our.Performance . . . End.Transmission."

If the crowd was going wild before, they were absolutely out of control at that moment. A couple of parents had to pull a goblin kid out of the rafters.

Griff rushed over to the band as Allie was powering down her Sonic Explodinator and Erik was putting his keyboard in its travel case. "You guys were palpable! Do you have any merch?"

Erik reached into the box and shyly held out a spoon.

"Whoooooaaaa! I've never heard of a band selling wooden spoons before!"

"Um . . . exactly?"

VLAD's BIZ BITES

Fun Fact: You can make any shirt into a beautiful, super-custom VLAD & THE MAGGOTS shirt.

All you need is a shirt, a permanent marker, and a guardian's permission.

If there's already something on the shirt, turn it inside out.

Then write VLAD & THE MAGGOTS really big on it.

Go over it a few times so it's nice and dark.

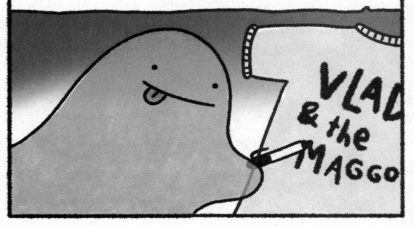

Dear Elise,

   I hope you're having a great day. What is the weather like there? It's gloomy and kinda dark here, but you probably would have guessed that. It's bright and warm in the greenhouse, though!

   Question: Have you ever had a reallyreallyreally fresh carrot before? Wow!

Love,
Quade

Dear Bestie,
I'm still VERY upset that you
had to go home. I screamed
into my Bad Feelings pillow so
hard that... well, it's a Bad
Feelings pile of ashes now. I
can't help but think that you
owe me one Bad Feelings pillow.
I've included a page from a
catalog with a couple of
options circled. COME BACK
(with the pillow)!!!
Love forever or else,
Lizzie

SOGGY LORE PRESS

hereby calls for your

SUBMISSION

to an upcoming volume of

POETRY by YOUNG BARDS.

Submit thine efforts to Gilly (publisher & editor).

Payment for inclusion:
- 1 meteorite (approx. 3 grams)
- 10 copies of published book

POETS WHO
KNOW IT

Gilly slapped a piece of paper on the bulletin board. "Behold," she declaredth. Everyone gathered around.

"Hmm . . . what's *Soggy Lore Press*?" gurfled Bobby.

"I be starting a publishing house, says I," said Gilly. "I seek to publish works by undiscovered writers and artists."

"I'm completely undiscovered," said Griff. "Count me in."

Lizzie scoffed. "An entire book of *poems*? Poems are just rhyming gibberish."

"Poems need not rhyme," said Gilly. "Verily, some of mine favorite–"

"Yeah, but the best and funniest ones rhyme," said Griff.

"The quality of poems, as with all art, be subjective," said Gilly.

"What be *subjective*?" asked Vlad.

"It means it's a matter of personal opinion," replied Frankie.

"But Gilly is deciding which poems get into her book, so she's the subjective-er," said Griff.

"Aye," said Gilly. "Good luck."

The submissions trickled in over the next few days. Some applicants were expected. Griff had expressed interest from the beginning, and Erik wrote poems and song lyrics pretty much every day.

A couple of entries surprised Gilly, however. When Emma (who didn't do much more than groan) handed Gilly a stained piece of parchment, Gilly read it over . . . and shed a small tear. And when Lizzie chucked a folded-up sheet of paper at Gilly's head, Gilly assumed it was just Lizzie being Lizzie. But when Lizzie shot Gilly her best *hey, that's important* look, Gilly picked up the paper, unfolded it, and discovered that it was a poem.

"Forsooth, Lizzie," said Gilly. "This poem be quite–"

"It's crud!" roared Lizzie. "I know! Just forget it!"

Two weeks later, Gilly brought an old shoe-box to school. She sat it down on the edge of the sandbox and took off the lid. Inside were bundles of tiny books. She handed the tied stacks to Emma, Erik, Griff, Bobby, Lobo, and Lizzie, along with small black chunks of iron. Then she set out a little sign

Little Books

Size 1

and fanned out individual copies of *Soggy Verses, Vol. 1.*

Griff untied his bundle and flipped through the top copy. "Wow! My first published piece!" He tossed and caught his meteorite. "I feel my future unfolding before me."

Vlad approached Gilly's makeshift storefront. "These are the books, eh?"

Gilly nodded and held out a copy. "Aye. Would ye like to get one?"

"There aren't very many pages. Are you sure this qualifies as a *book*?"

"How many pages be required to decree something a book?" asked Gilly.

"I . . . do . . . not know," replied Vlad.

"Call it a book, call it a magazine, call it a zine, call it a pamphlet," mused Gilly. "Call it whatever ye like. Just call it . . . thine?"

"Yeah, I'll take one."

SOGGY VERSES vol. 1

Collected Works
by Young Bards

Featuring "The Floobler"
by Lizzie

SOGGY LORE PRESS

Gilly's House, Creep's Cove

All works © by their respective authors, verily.

All rights reserved and other trifling legalese.

First printing

1 3 5 7 9 10 8 6 4 2

MY FRIEND

When I find I'm all alone
With lots of time to spend
I find a quiet hilly spot
And play with my best friend.
I toss a rock way up the hill.
She rolls it back to me.
It always helps me settle down.
She's my friend Gravity.

—by Emma

COUNTING LEGS

A centipede crept across the floor.

It paused to eat some ants.

I counted 15 pairs of legs

And zero pairs of pants.

—by Bobby

SMUDGE

Wet dead leaves
      leave dead wet smudges
To frayed white gloves.
      Nothing is truly felt
            by calloused fingers
                  underneath.

Wet dead leaves
      soak through
Two frayed white gloves
      To aching hands
            pounding keys
                  wiping damp dust.

      It's so dark in here.

—by Erik

TOMMY

This little boy named Tommy
Ate nothing but salami.
     Came from his pores
     A stinky force
That frightened off his mommy.

—by Griff

THE FLOOBLER

Flibble dibble plooble dee
I saw the Floobler in a tree.
Blibble skibble plibble deet
I chased the Floobler down the street.
Flabble dabble flarble plown
I ran the Floobler out of town.
Pibble flibble yibble flince
Nobody's seen the Floobler since.

—by Lizzie

Lizzie held her books with her eyes wide. "What? *Featuring* 'The Floobler' by Lizzie?"

"'Tis a spectacular piece of writing," said Gilly.

Lizzie blinked and stammered for a moment. "It's . . . just a bunch of gibberish, though."

"Aye, perhaps," said Gilly. "But gibberish with a purpose. Gibberish with heart. Many a creature hath spent a lifetime trying and failing to strike such a balance. Congratulations, Lizzie."

Lizzie looked at her stack of tiny books and her meteorite. "Well, um, the next one is gonna cost you *two* meteorites."

"Ah, there she be," laughed Gilly.

MOVING ON

obo's grandmother Lupina lived at Droopy Pines, a retirement community on the west side of Creep's Cove.

Oh. We should start over. You see, Lobo's grandmother didn't *live* anywhere. She was a ghost. So were about half the residents of Droopy Pines.

Lobo didn't really have much in common with his grandmother. He was a kid; she was an old lady. He was a werewolf; she was a ghost of a werewolf. He was shy and quiet;

she was the loudest person in just about any room. But they were best friends.

Lobo's family visited on weekends, but Lobo also stopped by after school once or twice a week. They'd talk about what Lobo learned that day and look at old photos. Lobo would eat his grandmother's favorite foods and describe the taste, and Lupina would close her eyes and smile at the memories. They'd listen to old-timey music from Lupina's huge record collection, and they'd practice old-timey dances together.

Recently, however, Lobo noticed that his grandmother would often look out the window and let conversations drift away. She wasn't as chatty as she used to be.

One particularly quiet afternoon, Lobo asked his grandmother if everything was okay.

"Oh, everything is fine, dear," said Lupina. "I tell you, the older I got when I was alive, the less the little unpleasant things mattered. Then, in my afterlife, I truly cherished the things that mattered even more. My family, good music, a hearty howl, the crackle of a juicy bug hitting the zapper. But now . . . I suppose that's starting to slip away."

"What do you mean?" asked Lobo.

Lupina sighed. "Well, dear, I think it's time for me to move on."

"Move on? But you already moved on. You're dead."

"Well," said Lupina. "I mean move on to what's next."

Lobo squirmed in his seat. "What . . . *is* next?"

"I have a few notions," chuckled Lupina. "But I'm not too sure. It's calling to me, though. And I intend to answer this time."

Tears welled up in Lobo's eyes.

"But first," said Lupina, lifting up from her chair, "unfinished business. A ghost's whole reason for sticking around. You had just come along when my life ended, and I thought you were the best thing I'd ever seen. So I put my unfinished business aside for a little bit, and then a little bit more."

"What is it, Grandma?" asked Lobo. "A mystery? Revenge? Secret treasure?"

"A song."

"A song?"

Lupina floated over to her shelves of records. "I've always loved music. I've collected

albums
my whole life. But
I never did find the
recording of *the* song."

Lobo looked around
the room. There must have
been hundreds of albums
on her shelves. And there was
an old jukebox in the kitchen loaded

with music. "You probably have every song ever written in your whole life here."

Lupina laughed. "Close, I'd bet. But there's one I could never find. It goes like this." Lupina closed her eyes and sang a melody.

"Dah-dee daaaah, dah-dee daaaah. Dum-dah dwee-dah . . . doodle-doooo."

"That's pretty," said Lobo. I've never heard it before."

"And I haven't heard it in so long," replied Lupina. "I'd like to hear it just once more if I can."

"I have a couple of ideas," said Lobo, scratching at his chin thoughtfully, but also at a flea. "Let's go see some friends of mine."

Lobo and Lupina stepped/floated out into the hallway. A swaying ghost cruised back and forth between the kitchen and dining room, smashing plates and vases as he went.

"Hello, Mr. Sterling," said Lobo.

"What do you waaaaaant?" groaned Mr. Sterling.

"Have you ever heard this song?" asked Lobo.

"Dah-dee daaaah, dah-dee daaaah. Dum-dah dwee-dah . . . doodle-doooo."

"REVEEEEEENGE!" moaned Mr. Sterling.

"Don't mind Mr. Sterling, dear," said Lupina. "Revenge is all he can think about. But that's *his* unfinished business. Who are we going to see?"

"I have two ideas," said Lobo. "First, let's go see Emma. Her mom is *super* old. She's probably heard a billion songs."

"Your names?" The butler at Emma's house was a seven-foot-tall ghoul with an obviously drawn-on mustache. He leaned

over and glared at Lobo and Lupina with a snobby, snooty look. Or maybe that was just his face.

"Lobo and Lupina Crowe," said Lobo. "I go to school with Emma."

"One moment." The butler slammed the door in the werewolves' faces.

A minute later, Emma opened the door. "HIIIIIIIII," she groaned.

"Hi, Emma! This is my grandmother."

"Pleased to meet you, darling," said Lupina.

Emma nodded.

"Emma, is your mom home?" asked Lobo. "We have a question for her."

"YYYYYYEEEEESSSSS," groaned Emma. She turned and motioned for Lobo and Lupina to follow. Emma led them to a blood-red door with a small window. She pressed a button next to it, and the door opened. Inside the small room, the butler stood next to a large wooden wheel.

"Going up?" he asked. It really was hard to tell if he was acting snobby or if he just *looked* snobby. The mustache was confusing.

The butler pushed the door closed and began cranking the wheel. The elevator creaked and began to ascend. Floor after floor passed by the little window. Bedrooms, a kitchen, workshops where spears and axes were being hammered and sharpened by gigantic armored beetles.

The elevator screeched to a halt. The butler sneered at Lobo. "Top floor, *peasants*." It was settled. The butler was snobby.

The door opened, and a patchy gray carpet led down a torchlit path to steps and a cobweb-covered throne. Between two rows of masked guards sat Emma's mother, Goddess-Queen Nefermetum.

Lobo, Lupina, and Emma approached. The guards stiffened.

Yikes, thought Lobo. *Do I bow? Avert my*

gaze or what-
ever?

"Well, hello,
Lobo!"

Lobo
looked up.
Through
Emma's mom's
wraps, he could
almost detect a
smile.

"Hello,   um,
Queen . . . Your Majesty . . . um . . ."

"Oh, hush," said the Queen. "And who
might this fellow Lady of the Undead be?"

"Hello there, Your Majesty. Lupina Crowe.
I'm the young squire's grandmother."

Queen Nefermetum motioned for her
guards to stand at ease. "And what can I do
for you two?"

"My grandmother is trying to find this

old song she loves. And I thought that, well,
since you're—"

"SOOO OOOOOOLD," groaned Emma.

"Um . . ." Lobo squirmed.

"Go on," said the Queen.

"You've been around for a while," said
Lobo. "So maybe you've heard it. It goes like,

Dah-dee daaaah, dah-dee daaaah."

Lupina joined in.

**"Dum-dah dwee-dah . . .
doodle-doooo."**

Emma swayed to the music.

"Have you heard it?" asked Lobo.

"I don't believe I have," said the Queen. "It's lovely, though. I hope you find it."

"PRRRRRRETTTYYYYY," groaned Emma.

A gigantic beetle wearing chain mail scuttled through the doors and bowed at the throne. He held out a scroll, and the Queen snatched it out of his claws. She unrolled the scroll, looked it over, wadded it up, and chucked it at the beetle's head.

"I said two thousand axes by the end of the month. How are we so off track?"

The beetle groveled.

Queen Nefermetum turned back to Lobo and Lupina. "Apologies, but duty calls. Good luck with your unfinished business, Lupina. I know something of that myself."

"Indeed," said Lupina with a floaty curtsy. "Lovely to meet you."

"Okay, this is my other thought," said Lobo. "This guy is the most musical kid I know. Maybe he's heard your song."

Lobo knocked on Erik's garage door. Chaotic, desperately sad music was pounding from inside. Lobo knocked harder, and the music stopped.

The door creaked open, and Erik waved hello. Allie was in the back of the garage tuning her Sonic Explodinator.

"Oh, sorry, Erik. Didn't know you were having a Vlad and the Maggots practice. Great show at Griff's party, by the way."

"Thanks," said Erik. "I mean, it's more like an . . . *and the Maggots* practice. Vlad is out scouting locations for an, as he put it, *epic video album.* So we're trying to come up with a few more songs for it."

"Speaking of songs— Oh, I'm sorry. This is my grandmother."

"Nice to meet you, madame," said Erik.

"Hello, dear. Nice racket you're making in there!"

"Thanks!"

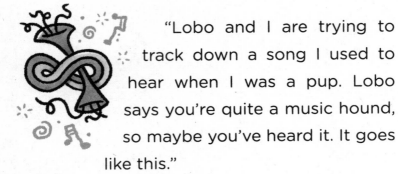

"Lobo and I are trying to track down a song I used to hear when I was a pup. Lobo says you're quite a music hound, so maybe you've heard it. It goes like this."

Lobo and Lupina sang the melody together.

"Dah-dee daaaah, dah-dee daaaah. Dum-dah dwee-dah . . . doodle-doooo."

"Have you heard it?" asked Lobo.

"No, never—but it's really nice," said Erik. "Can we use it?"

Lobo was disappointed that neither of his ideas had panned out, but suddenly he had another thought. "The library! I don't know why I didn't think of that first!"

"Lead the way," said Lupina.

The library on Creep's Cove was a winding labyrinth where the books were arranged by spine color. If you asked the librarian, Mrs. Vivlio, it was the best and *only* way to properly organize a library.

The music collection in the basement of the library had a different system. Mrs. Vivlio believed that the most important element to any song was the drummer, so the records, CDs, cassettes, PocketVerses,* discs, etc. were

---

* POCKETVERSES WERE A SHORT-LIVED MUSIC STORAGE FORMAT WHERE SONGS WERE STORED IN TEENY-TINY UNIVERSES. THEY WERE DISCONTINUED AFTER ONLY A FEW YEARS FOLLOWING A NUMBER OF RIPS IN THE SPACE-TIME CONTINUUM.

sorted alphabetically by the drummer's first name. Since Lupina was pretty sure there *wasn't* a drummer on the song they were looking for, their search would be limited to the drummer-less section, meaning it would be a lot easier to potentially find what they were looking for.

Lupina and Lobo made their way down the spiral staircase to the basement. "Okay, Grandma," said Lobo. "The drummer-less section is to the right of the entrance, so we can—"

"Help you find something?" It was Mrs. Vivlio, who had suddenly appeared from a hole in the wall.

"Hi, Mrs. Vivlio," said Lobo. "We're trying to find a song. It doesn't have a drummer, so we were going to check the—"

"We have a new system," interrupted Mrs. Vivlio. "It's important to keep up with changes in technology, you see."

"I see," said Lobo.

Mrs. Vivlio opened the double doors to the music section. Where racks of recordings once lined long wooden shelves, Lobo was shocked to see a floor-to-ceiling array of fuzzy white cables and what looked like deflated basketballs. One of the orange floppy discs burst and sprayed yellow powder in every direction. "Presenting . . . the Fungal Sonic Net!" announced Mrs. Vivlio.

"Fungal?" asked Lobo. "Like fungus? Mushrooms?"

"Smartest network technology on earth," replied Mrs. Vivlio. She looked *very* proud.

"How does it work?" asked Lupina.

Mrs. Vivlio tapped a nearby mushroom. It swung over to Lobo and Lupina, tilted toward their faces, and curved into a slight bowl. "Tell the Fungal Sonic Net what music you're looking for."

"We don't know the name of it," said Lobo. "That's the problem."

Mrs. Vivlio tapped one of her horns thoughtfully. "Can you hum or sing part of it?"

"That's all we *can* do," chuckled Lupina.

"Then you don't have a problem," said Mrs. Vivlio. "Go ahead."

Lobo and Lupina leaned in to the eagerly listening mushroom.

"Dah-dee daaaah, dah-dee daaaah. Dum-dah dwee-dah ... doodle-doooo."

The mush-room quivered. The array of white strands pulsed and wiggled. Spores burst from a few mushroom caps. From deep in the basement, Lobo and Lupina could hear rustling and scrounging.

Suddenly, a thick strand of fungus burst out of the ground. Wrapped in its tendrils was a stack of records.

"Ah, looks like you have a few potential matches," mused Mrs. Vivlio. "The Fungal Sonic Net is a TRUE WONDER of organization and information! Record players are to the left. Library closes in fifteen minutes." The minotaur smiled at the Fungal Sonic Net and leapt through a hole in the ceiling.

Lobo and Lupina took the records to the listening station and tried them out. Lupina's song wasn't on any of them.

Lobo and Lupina walked slowly back to Droopy Pines as the smoggy glow began to dwindle

ahead of them. Lobo felt defeated, but Lupina had a strange, pleasant smile on her face. She was almost twinkling.

Back in her room, Lupina floated over to her chair by the window.

"I'm so sorry, Grandma," said Lobo. "I really tried. I guess your business is still unfinished."

"No," replied Lupina. "I believe we figured it out."

"How?"

"That song . . . I suppose it was never recorded. It was something *my* grand-mother used to sing

and hum while we cooked together, while we went on walks, and when she tucked me in when I'd stay at her house in the summer."

"Do you know who wrote it?"

"Well," said Lupina, "I guess *she* did? Or nobody did. It was just one of those silly little melodies that comes out when you're really living. And what matters is the feeling, not just the notes."

"So you can't hear it again?"

"Lobo, I got to hear it and sing that old song all day with you. Thank you."

Lobo sniffled. "So does that mean—"

"Yes, dear. It's time for me to answer that call."

Lobo let out a sob.

"Now, now," said Lupina. "I really did all there is and then some. I raced through the woods and let the branches scratch at my skin. I stole chickens from terrified farmers. I was the scourge of an entire village."

"Really?" whimpered Lobo. "The . . . the scourge?"

"Indeed. I had a terrific life *and* a terrific afterlife. Most people don't become ghosts, you know. I'm glad we got this extra time."

"Me too," said Lobo. "But I'm going to miss you."

"I'm going to miss you, too," said Lupina. "But I won't be far. Look for me peeking just over the horizon. Look for the fangs flickering in the darkness behind the darkness. That's me snarling at you."

The lights in the bedroom dimmed. The wind chimes outside the window clinked in a growing breeze.

Lupina smiled. "Howl at the moon, Lobo. Dig in the dirt with your claws, and run as hard as you can until your lungs burn. Live a ridiculous, terrifying, wild, powerful life."

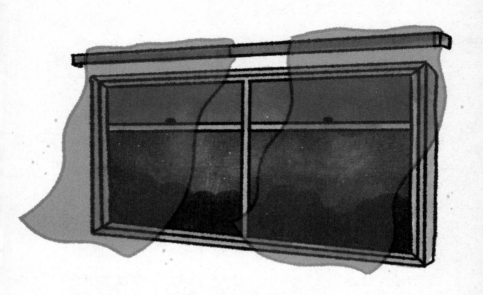

Lobo's grandmother turned to the window. The night pulled at her, called to her. She slipped into it.

Two weeks later, Lobo's family and friends stood in a circle on the smoggy beach surrounding a collection of instruments, speakers, machinery, and cables. Adam approached with spool of wire, unwinding it as he walked.

"This oughta do it," said Adam. "Hooked it up to a goblin generator back at the harbor. They said it's fueled by 'little-kid nightmares' or somethin'. Let's check it out." He handed Frankie the plug at the end of the wire.

Frankie plugged the wire into the back of a control box, and a sharp buzz burst from the speakers. A few light bulbs in the machinery glowed green.

"Those are some baaaaaad nightmares," said Frankie. "Looks like we're all set. Lobo?"

Lobo stepped to the middle of the circle and stood behind a microphone.

"Thanks for coming, everyone," said Lobo. "This is a celebration of life and after-life. For those of us here and those of us *sort of* here—"

"WOOO!" wooed a small crowd of ghosts.

"And those of us in the next . . . wherever," said Lobo. "Grab some food. We've got a buffet courtesy of Mogwai's Wok, some treats from Andy's Candies—"

"ANDREW'S Candies!" shouted Andrew.

"Oh, sorry. And, uh, yeah. Let's have

some fun. I'd like to welcome Vlad and the Maggots, who are allowing me to play a song with them."

Vlad, Allie, and Erik joined Lobo in the center of the circle.

"This is going to be an epic scene for the video album," whispered Vlad. "I've got Bobby and Quade on camera duty."

Vlad tapped a button on a super-dangerous-looking box of bulbs and wires, and a puls-ing beat boomed through the speakers. "Let's wake the neighbors!" he shouted.

Erik played a few notes; then Lobo began to sing.

"Dah-dee daaaah, dah-dee daaaah."

The crowd danced to the music. Erik noodled on the keys in a skillful but not-too-show-off-y way.

"Dum-dah dwee-dah . . . doodle-doooo."

Allie looked to Lobo, and Lobo glanced up. Allie pointed her Sonic Explodinator toward the sky and pounded on two large buttons. With a **FWOOOOOOM** and a haunting chord,* a shock wave shot straight out of Allie's instrument.

A fifty-foot-wide hole burst open in the smog overhead, revealing a full moon and

---

* THE CHORD ALLIE PLAYED TO BURST THE SKY OPEN WAS AN E-FLAT MAJOR 7. PLEASE BE CAREFUL WHAT YOU DO WITH THIS INFORMATION.

starry sky. The werewolves in attendance immediately started howling.

Everyone else joined in.

A werepenguin wearing pajamas and holding a flashlight waddled out onto the beach. "What's the meaning of all of this racket? We're trying to sl—"

The werepenguin looked up and saw the full moon and immediately began squeaking and squawking at it. He dropped his flashlight and flapped his little flippers.

"Cute!" yelled Lizzie. "AWOOOOOOO!!!"

Out of the corner of the *corner* of Lobo's eye, he thought he caught a flash of fangs in the bushes. He snarled back at it.

Welcome to *Terrible Friends*, the show where we bring side characters front and center. I'm your host, Quade.

Joining me are three beings with small roles, but huge impacts.

147

Great! Also joining us is Robbi, Bobby's younger sibling.

Hi, Quade!

Robbi, the "annoying little sister" role...

150

154

Oooookay.

Question for the group.

Do you wish you played a larger role in the Terribles series?

157

Says here that Nuan likes opera...

...and "ruining magic shows."

See you next time.

Kinda mean to ruin a magic show, right?

GNOMES
UNDERFOOT, PART 2

Frankie, Dr. Shelley (Frankie's dad), and Lobo stood on the pier as an adorable, elaborately carved wooden ship sailed into the harbor. Lobo was asked to be there because of his strong sense of smell, and

he was on a leash held by Dr. Shelley just in case of an urge to, you know, rip someone apart.

Adam, wearing a super-authentic fisherman's sweater, strolled out of the harbor office and over to the docks. "Hey, Ma. Hey, Grandpa. Fine day for it, eh?"

The boat slid up to the dock, and two golden ropes were tossed from the deck. Adam tied the boat to the dock's cleats and waved up at the tips of colorful hats peeking over the side. He strolled back to the harbor office, whistling. "Holler if you need me," he said.

A ladder slid down from the side of the boat and met the dock. A gnome wearing a bright green dress (and,

obviously, a pointy hat) stepped over and climbed down. As she walked toward the greeting party, Lobo noticed a cheery smile through her thick beard.

A smaller gnome hopped down and ran up next to her. He nervously looked around and stayed close to the adult.

"You must be Mrs. Chamomile," said Dr. Shelley, bending over and extending his hand.

The gnome smiled and shook his index finger. "Dr. Shelley. It's a pleasure. And you must be Frankie and Lobo. This is my son, Basil."

The kids greeted each other shyly.

"Right. First things first," said Dr. Shelley. "Lobo?"

Lobo nodded and took a step forward. He sniffed Mrs. Chamomile and Basil, then gave Dr. Shelley a thumbs-up.

"It appears your scent-blocking cream works just fine, Doctor," said Mrs. Chamomile.

Dr. Shelley motioned to Frankie, who pulled a few tiny bottles from her lab coat pocket. "And we've just come out with a new product. Scent-blocking spray. Easier application. Everyone should reapply every three hours to be extra safe."

"Oh, how lovely," said Mrs. Chamomile. "Thank you very much." Then she turned to the boat and whistled.

Six gnome kids and a couple of adults climbed down from the boat and lined up.

They greeted the humans and werewolf as they passed by. Lobo sniffed them one by one and nodded at Dr. Shelley.

When a slumpy-hatted, stubble-faced gnome passed, however, Lobo perked up and flashed his fangs. "Ummmm . . . I'm sorry," he growled. "But I kinda want to scratch this kid's face off. No offense."

Mrs. Chamomile scowled at the gnome-smelling gnome. "Sage, did you apply the cream?"

"I was gonna," he replied.

Mrs. Chamomile spritzed Sage with one of the bottles of scent-blocking spray.

"Arms. Turn. Eyes closed. There. Lobo, dear?"

Lobo leaned in and sniffed. "Nice to meet you, Sage. I'm Lobo."

They shook hands.

The gnomes, along with their welcoming committee, approached the playground. Basil and Sage carried a small wooden trunk.

The Stubtoe Elementary kids introduced

themselves and went over their creepoball[*]
positions. Then it was the Longleaf Primary
kids' turn.

"Sage and Honeysuckle are our Goug-
ers," said Basil. Honeysuckle brushed her
long yellow hair out of her face and waved.

Two gnomes with matching smiles
stepped forward and talked in unison.
"We're Butternut and Cinnamon, and we're
the team Knotters."

"Are we baking a pie, or are we playing
creepoball?" snarled Lizzie.

A gnome with a cool scar across his
cheek cut through the crowd and stood in
front of Lizzie. He almost came up to her

---

* AS A REMINDER, CREEPOBALL WAS CREATED ON CREEP'S COVE
BY MIXING AND SMASHING TOGETHER VARIOUS SPORTS AND
GAMES PLAYED BY ALL MANNER OF NEW INHABITANTS OF THE
ISLAND. NO ONE UNDERSTANDS MORE THAN APPROXIMATELY
30 PERCENT OF THE GAME ALTOGETHER.

knee. "I'm going to make you eat more than a slice of your words," he said.

"I like this one," chuckled Lizzie.

"The name's Snakeroot," said the grizzled gnome. "Team Slacker."

"What a coincidence," said Lizzie. "I just this very second became our team Slacker. Lizzie."

They pounded fists.

"Coooooool," whispered Griff.

"Right," said Basil. "Moving on—I'm the team Slimer. And this is Persimmon, our Howler."

"That's me," said a rosy-cheeked, barefooted, lanky (for a gnome) gnome.

"Couple of problems,"

168

said Basil. "We don't have a Peeker or a Bubbler."

"Oh," said Frankie. "We don't, either."

"What's a Bubbler?" asked Erik.

"Not sure," said Persimmon. "Something about a bucket of old dishwater."

The kids all looked around at each other. "I guess we can skip it," ploffered Bobby.

After a few more minutes of small talk, Quade opened his team's creepoball equipment trunk. He held out two shovels to Sage and Honeysuckle. "I'm . . . not sure how . . ."

"That's okay," said Honeysuckle. "We have our own." Honeysuckle opened the gnomish trunk and pulled out two tiny shovels.

Gilly pulled a wooden ball out of the full-sized trunk. It was bigger than any of the gnomes. "And the orbs?"

Cinnamon jumped up and snatched the ball out of Gilly's hand. "We can handle it."

Mrs. Chamomile and Ms. Verne stepped/slithered out onto the field. "I'll send you the recipe," said Mrs. Chamomile. "Let me know what you think. Okay, kids! Who's ready for some **CREEPOBALL**?"

Everyone cheered. Honeysuckle and Vlad banged their shovels together.

Mrs. Chamomile blew a whistle. Immediate pandemonium ensued.

Snakeroot and Lizzie attacked the Snarl from either side. Lizzie found a loose end, but Snakeroot uncovered the first corner of the wagger. **"NOOOO!"** roared Lizzie.

Cinnamon and Emma chased after the skin orb. Emma tripped on a rock and lost a couple of toes.

Butternut grabbed the wind orb out of a tree, but it blew away.

Griff and Basil raced to glaze the slime orb, but they were knocked over by Erik and Sage. Erik tripped over a strand of the Snarl and tumbled halfway across the field.

Suddenly, a loud *THUUUUDDDD* echoed through the playground.

"THE WAGGER HAS BEEN UNCOVERED!" shouted Lizzie.

Ms. Verne flipped tiles on the scoreboard.

The fire orb slammed into the water orb, and steam hissed, covering half the field.

"Fourteen points!" shouted Persimmon.

"Begin.Transmission . . . Negative.The. Stone.Orb.Has.Not.Been.Fastened . . . End. Transmission," chirped Allie.

"Oh! Nine points!"

Gilly pounded the wood orb into the dirt. **"EARTHED!"**

It was swirling, piling chaos. Quade and Butternut fastened the wind orb to the slime orb and were knocked back by the blast.

"NOWWWWW!" groaned Emma.

Shovels, orbs, and twine were dropped, and everyone ran to the center of the field. Each kid shouted **BLINK** or **LAUGH** until they found an opponent shouting the same word. Then they bumped foreheads and took a step back.

Lobo blinked and fell to the ground. Quade laughed when Butternut made a fish face. Allie out-stared Persimmon, then moved on to Snakeroot. Lizzie blinked, then stormed off the field. Vlad sang *"There's a world inside my belly button, and it kiii-iiinda stinks"* in a high-pitched voice at Basil but made himself laugh instead. When

every player had finished three bouts, the field fell silent.

Everyone looked over at Ms. Verne and Mrs. Chamomile. They were calculating and flipping tiles on the scoreboard. Finally, they turned to the kids.

"Final score," said Mrs. Chamomile. "Longleaf Primary, forty-nine." She paused. "Stubtoe Elementary . . . fifty."

Everyone, even the gnomes, cheered and jumped around. Basil pulled a tiny trophy from their case and handed it to Frankie. The plaque on the front read CROSS-ARCHIPELAGO CUP CHAMPS.

The kids shared a big lunch of acorn soup, pickled things, stuffed peppers, nutrient cubes, spaghetti squash and tomato sauce, and swamp weed. Vlad offered Cinnamon a sip of his B negative, but they politely declined.

A few days later, Strudel tapped on a

window by the reading nook. Frankie opened the pane and took a parcel from Strudel's basket. She watched the bird hop over to a tree and hug a giant bat. They flew off together.

Frankie untied the string and tore off the paper. Inside was a thick sheet of parchment and a second piece of parchment folded in

half. The front of the folded
piece read COIN BOWL. Frankie
read the single sheet aloud.

Dear Pals,

That was loads of fun! Next time, perhaps
you'll want to play coin bowl against us.
Here's a rule book.

Quade unfolded the other piece of parchment. The "rule book" showed a picture of a
bowl and three coins.

HOW TO PLAY COIN BOWL:

Stand a little bit away from the bowl.
Try to throw coins into it.
Each coin that makes it into the bowl is
worth one point.

Take turns.
First person or team to get to ten points wins.

"Wait," said Vlad. "Could you also play this with pebbles and a circle drawn in sand?"

"Do you throw overhand or underhand?" asked Lobo.

"Could you change up the number of points for different sizes of bowls and different distances?" asked Erik.

"Couldst I stay inside and read instead?" asked Gilly.

"Ooh! Can you do, like, different trick shots?" asked Griff.

"Hmm," said Quade. "Not sure about any of that." He flipped the game book over. "Oh."

You can use a bowl and coins, or you can play with pebbles and a circle drawn in sand. You can throw overhand or underhand—your call. Also, you can change up the number of points for different bowl sizes and distances. Just have fun with it! Or just go inside and read if you want. But if you do play, you should absolutely try different trick shots.

"Well," said Lizzie. "This game makes zero sense."

Vlad leaned over and looked at the parchments. "Does it not say *anything* about shovels?"

"I guess we better get to work on their trophy," said Quade.

Visit the BiG Pile of JuNk

GARCUS J. TUPPY
MANAGER & CURATOR

Creep's Cove's Premiere Park for **CREATIVE FREEDOM.**

We'll give you the tools and parts. The rest is up to **YOU!** If you can carry, wheel, or fly it out, it's **YOURS.** Please take a lot.

Junk donations gladly accepted at the back gate. Just don't tell my auntie. She owns the lot and she says I gotta stop taking junk. It's...a problem.

Free admission. You gotta help us move some of this junk! PLEASE!

Brought to you in part by Muggy Chunks.
EAT MORE MUGGY CHUNKS. NOW.

THE BIG PILE OF JUNK

On a trip to the Big Pile of Junk, each student from Ms. Verne's older-ish class was given a hammer, a bag of nails, and a roll of tape. Then they were let loose in the park for a few hours. Let's see what everyone came up with.

ERIK'S STORM BUSTER

"I'm starting a new musical duo. It's me and the weather. Every element of this instrument is made to be played by untamed wind and water."

GRIFF'S 100-SIDED DIE

"Not only does this thing go from 1 to 50, it also has words and symbols and colors. No board game will EVER be the same."

LIZZIE'S SMALL
PILE OF JUNK

"My nails were the wrong size and my hammer was weird and the tape was too sticky. Nothing worked right. Here. Can we leave now?"

ALLIE'S NUTRIENT GOO FLAVORIZOR

"Begin.Transmission . . . This.
Device.Injects.Assorted.Flavor.
Profiles.Into.Rations.Of.Nutrient.
Goo.For.Gustatory.Delight . . .
End.Transmission."

GILLY'S WATERPROOF BOOKSHELF

"To all pesky drips from above, floods from below, and splashes from hither AND thither, I say to thee—NAY!"

LOBO'S OMNI-SCRATCHER

"For all of those hard-to-reach
places—at the same time."

EMMA'S WRAP STATION

"SORRRT."

VLAD'S COFFIN WEDGE

"Now I can prop my feet up higher than my head. All the good ideas will flow directly to my brain as I sleep. Frankie can back me up on the science. Frankie? Anyone know where Frankie is?"

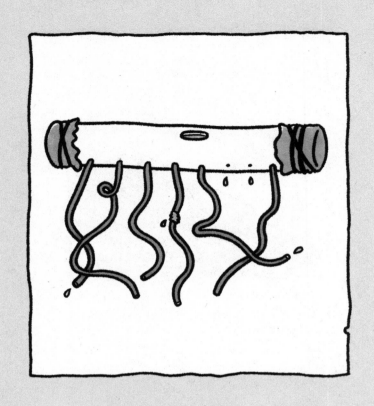

QUADE'S DRIP SYSTEM

"I nailed a bunch of holes in this pipe. Now I can water a whole row of plants at once."

BOBBY'S ACTION FIGURE DISPLAY

"A cubby for every figure I have, plus a bunch of empty ones. Leaving room to grow is the key to success. Right, Vlad?"

FRANKIE'S SHRINK RAY

"I made a shrinking ray. Um . . . can somebody please call my dad?"

Dear Quade,
Hello! It's actually kind of gloomy in Belgium right now, too. Reminds me of Creep's Cove a little bit. Yep! I've had reallyreally fresh carrots. My dad grows them. I'm including some turnip seeds. You'll know they're ready when they unbury themselves and hop onto your plate!
Hugs & slugs,
  Elise

Dear Lizzie,
Nice to hear from you! I'm sorry about your pillow. How about this—next time I visit, I'll do a spell to turn the ashes back into a pillow. It's a pretty simple spell. There's only a slight chance it'll turn you into an egg. Just keep the ashes in a box or something. Until then, I hope you find safer ways to sort out your feelings. (I miss you too.)
Hugs & Bugs & Slugs,
  Elise

THE PERFECT DAY.
AGAIN!

Lizzie woke up to the smell and sound of grilling fish. She leapt out of bed and stomped into the kitchen.

"Brown sauce?" she asked. **"BROWN SAUCE?!"**

"Brown sauce," said her mom (the flying one).

"Nothing beats it," said her mom (the non-flying one).

Lizzie and her moms pounded filet after

filet drenched in the family's *top-secret* brown sauce recipe.[*]

"Ahhhh," said Lizzie. "That was perfect. Can I go to the park now?"

"Sure," said Lizzie's mom (the flying one).

---

* TO MAKE THIS BROWN SAUCE AT HOME, POUR 1 CUP OF— HEY. WHAT PART OF TOP SECRET DON'T YOU UNDERSTAND?

"I've got to get to my daily routine of flying around the island and screeching at the great farce we call existence. I'll give you a ride."

"And I'll just be here," said Lizzie's mom (the non-flying one). "Cleaning up the kitchen, then burrowing deep into the earth to plot and scheme."

"Have fun!" roared Lizzie.

Lizzie and her mom (the flying one) raced through the sky. "I wish I could fly." Lizzie sighed.

Lizzie's mom (the flying one, obviously)

tore through the treetops and ripped a power line from a pole. "Who knows, dear. Maybe you'll go through another larval stage and grow wings. At any rate, I can always give you a lift."

"I the opposite of hate you, Mom."

"I the opposite of hate you, too, dear. Now . . . don't forget . . . to ROLL!"

Lizzie's mom (the flying one) opened her claws and dropped Lizzie. Lizzie hit the ground and tumbled. She came out of her somersault and stood up directly in front of Bobby and Frankie.

"That was PERFECT!" chorbled Bobby.

"Game shop?" asked Lizzie.

"Game shop," agreed Frankie.

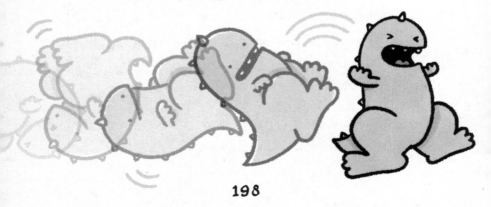

Biscuits, the owner of Absolute Pile of Games and one of the island's few reverse centaurs, whinnied and clapped his hooves when he saw some of his favorite customers.

"Do you got 'em?" asked Lizzie.

"Indeeeeeed I do!" neighed Biscuits. "Series 3 of T.U.F.F. Squad™ Baddleboos!"

"Three packs, please," said Lizzie.

"That'll be fifteen cubes," Biscuits neighed.

Frankie, the only kid with pockets, pulled

out a small box. She carefully counted fifteen sugar cubes and slid them across the counter.

Biscuits whinnied in approval.

The kids rushed outside and opened their packs. A couple of Lizzie's cards were pretty basic, but she also pulled two new heroes with six Clout points each and a Bone Shield Pile-On.

"Luckyyyyyyy," glorfed Bobby.

Frankie handed Bobby and

Lizzie small plastic sleeves. "Here," she said. "Let's keep those cards in mint condition." Lizzie and Bobby slid their new cards into the sleeves and handed them back to Frankie, who put them in a lab coat pocket for safekeeping.

Just then, Emma and Quade came around the corner carrying cardboard boxes.

"Hey, pals!" called Quade. "Muffin?"

Quade and Emma opened the lids to their boxes, revealing rows of assorted, colorful lumps.

"Wow! What are these for?" asked Frankie.

Quade gave everyone a napkin. "We're taking these down to Droopy Pines, but we baked extra."

"MUFFFINNNNS," groaned Emma.

Lizzie grabbed a muffin topped with tan clumps.

"Good choice," Quade said. "That's ginger-cranberry with a crumble."

It was the most perfect muffin Lizzie ever had.

As Lizzie licked her fingers, a moth fluttered over and landed on her forehead. It delicately touched its mouth between her eyes, then darted away.

"It kissed me!" Lizzie giggled. "It kissed me!"

The next day, Lizzie woke up to a sharp pain in her side. She rolled over and found a Dino Rusty action figure on her mattress. **"AAAAUUUUUGGG!"**

Lizzie chucked the toy at the wall. Its head popped off.

"Great," she grumbled.

Lizzie stomped into an empty kitchen. Lizzie's mom (the non-flying one) popped her head out of her burrow. "Hey, kiddo! Your mom's off flying and tormenting, but we made porridge."

Lizzie opened the fridge to find a bowl of gray-brown gruel. She took a bite and sighed. It was . . . porridge.

Lizzie wandered around the park, but she didn't see any of her friends. Not even any of her enemies. She trudged over to Absolute Pile of Games, but it was closed.

What an incredibly crummy day, she thought.

Thunder cracked overhead, and Lizzie was immediately drenched in a downpour of rain.

She kicked a rock. It really, really hurt.

The next day, Lizzie gathered her class-mates together at recess. "Listen up, everyone. I had the PERFECT day this weekend."

"Oh, that's really nice," said Lobo.

"LET ME FINISH," roared Lizzie. "I had the **PERFECT** day this weekend. So, like anyone would in my position, I tried to have it *exactly* again."

"Did it work?" asked Vlad.

"It did not," said Lizzie.

Bobby fiffed through his T.U.F.F. Squad™ Baddleboos cards. "Well, sometimes things just don't work out. Should we—"

"Things **ALWAYS** work out," growled Lizzie. "I will have my perfect day again. And you're all going to help me."

Lizzie described, in excruciating detail, her perfect day. She assigned everyone

specific tasks. For those she encountered in the original version, they were told to re-create their performances exactly as before. Others were given jobs such as traffic control, moth wrangling, and fruit services.

"And what about me?" asked Griff.

"I need you to be my day-of coordinator," said Lizzie.

"What's that?" asked Griff.

"Your job is to rush around and make sure everyone is where they're supposed to be and doing what they're supposed to be doing."

Griff pumped his fists in the air. Nobody saw. "PALPABLE! Can I wear a headset?"

"No headset. Just scamper around and keep things in line."

"Got it. I feel like I want to wear a headset, though."

Lizzie smiled through clenched jaws. "Nobody else will be wearing a headset, so it doesn't really make sense."

"Yeah, I'm going to wear a headset."

Lizzie felt a little ball of fire rumbling around inside her. She took a breath and felt it cool down. "Whatever. Just . . . can you handle this?"

"Oh, you can count on me, chumarino."

"Great."

"And I'm definitely going to wear a headset."

"Fine."

Griff paused. "Hey, Frankie. Do you know where I could get a headset?"

The group rehearsed every day that week during recess. It was loose at first.

"Nonono—you come by with the muffins AFTER the game shop."

But slowly . . .

"Smoosh the little piece of old fruit right here. RIGHT HERE. Otherwise the moth won't land right."

. . . it came together.

"I think we got it. Great. From the top, people!"

Lizzie woke up to the sound and smell of grilling kelp. She leapt out of bed and stomped into the kitchen.

"Brown sauce?" she asked. "Wait . . . where's the brown sauce?

"Trying something a little different," announced Lizzie's mom (the non-flying one). "Green sauce!"

Lizzie squinted and slowly sat down at the table. Her mom (the flying one) put a bowl in front of her. She took a bite. It was . . . pretty good.

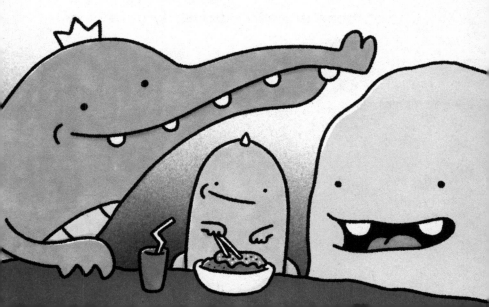

"It's different," said Lizzie.

"Yeah," said Lizzie's mom (the non-flying one). "It needs . . . something. Well, I tried."

Lizzie and her moms slurped down their breakfast. Then Lizzie stood up and asked, "Can I go to the park now?"

"Sure," said Lizzie's mom (the non-flying one). "I'll dig you there."

Lizzie and her mom (the non-flying one) burrowed through the earth toward the park. Rocks, roots, bones, treasure chests, giant ants, more bones, veins of goo, and pipes rushed by. Suddenly, the pair made a sharp turn upward and burst to the surface. Lizzie's head popped up directly in front of Gilly and Frankie.

A voice coming from the direction of a floating headset called out from ten feet away. **"ACTION!"**

Frankie smiled and waved. "Hey, Lizzie!"

Lizzie looked around. "Wait, where's Bobby?"

"Verily," said Gilly. "Bobby had to help his mother at her restaurant."

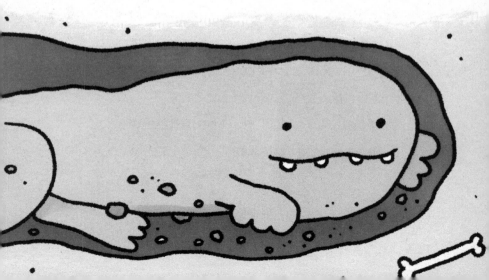

Lizzie scowled and huffed. "But that's not what happened last week. Let's . . . let's just keep it moving."

Lizzie, Gilly, and Frankie walked to Absolute Pile of Games. Biscuits clapped his hooves and whinnied when they entered.

"Do you got 'em?" asked Lizzie.

Biscuits scratched his horse chin with his man arm. "What, the new Baddleboos? Yeah, you got some last week."

"The line is *Indeed I do,* Biscuits!" whispered Griff.

"Indeeeeed I do!" neighed Biscuits.

"Three packs, please," said Lizzie.

"That'll be fifteen cubes," neighed Biscuits.

Frankie counted fifteen sugar cubes and slid them across the counter.

Biscuits whinnied in approval.

The kids rushed outside and opened their packs.

"What the heck is this?" growled Lizzie. Instead of Series 3 T.U.F.F. Squad™ Baddle-boos cards, her pack was full of brightly colored Snail Pals Baddleboos cards. She kicked the door open, stomped back into the game shop, and slammed the cards down on the counter.

"Oh," whinnied Biscuits. "Looks like there was a mix-up at the printer. They're compatible games, though. Anyway, you can trade them in for a new pack."

"Hold it." Lizzie picked up the top card from the stack of Snail Pals cards and looked it over. "**EIGHT** Clout points? And a

213

Grit Multiplier?!" She flipped through the cards. "Shell of Steel? Slime Dancer? These are compatible?"

Biscuits stomped and nodded. "All series of Baddleboos cards are playable with each other. Did you want to . . . ?"

"I'll keep them. Or whatever. I don't care." Lizzie grabbed the cards and turned to Frankie. "Sleeve?"

Frankie took the cards from Lizzie and slipped the cards into a plastic sleeve, then tucked them in a lab coat pocket.

Lizzie, Gilly, and Frankie stepped outside.

"Cue the muffins!" shouted Griff.

Emma and Quade approached from stage left holding two boxes. Lizzie smiled and lifted one of the lids. Her smile dropped.

"Where's the ginger-cranberry?

"Sorry, Lizzie," said Quade. "We used all the cranberries last week. These have crab-apple, and these have currants."

There was a rustling from above. Lobo dropped down from a branch and landed on Lizzie's head. He smooshed an old berry on Lizzie's forehead and scampered away.

"MOTH!" shouted Griff.

"The shouting is pretty distracting," said Frankie.

"Verily," said Gilly.

"HEEEAAADDDSEETSS," groaned Emma.

"Totally," said Frankie. "We should have all had headsets."

215

Vlad rolled out of a bush holding a large cardboard box. He opened the lid, and an ENORMOUS moth whooshed out.

"WHAT IS THAT?!" roared Lizzie.

"It's a moth!" beamed Vlad. "I got the most epic one I could find so your day would be extra—"

"IT'S EATING MY FACE! IT'S EATING MY FACE!"

Lizzie rolled around on the ground and flailed her little arms, the moth flapping

and frantically slurping at the old berry on her forehead. The moth snatched it and launched back into the air and over the horizon.

Lizzie lay facedown and panting on the ground. Vlad and Lobo slowly crept over. Erik and Allie nodded at each other and ran home. A single drop of rain hit Lizzie on the back of the head. Frankie looked up at the sky.

"We . . . are . . . in . . . danger," said Frankie.

The clouds exploded with rain and soaked the park and everyone in it. Lizzie slowly sat up. A growl grew from inside her. Everyone else took a step back.

Lizzie's growl turned into a roar. She threw back her head, and her roar rolled into hearty laughter. She stood up and stomped in a puddle, then kicked muddy water toward Gilly. Gilly smiled and kicked water back.

Frankie growled and splashed Vlad. Lobo roared and splashed Emma. Everyone stomped, laughed, roared, and danced in the soggy mess of a perfectly ruined perfect day.

How to Play
HOW DARE YOU ASK ME THAT?!

HOW DARE YOU ASK ME THAT?! is a fun and casual card game for the whole family (two to four players). On Creep's Cove, it's played with a four-suited deck of cards that's pretty similar to the fifty-two-card deck you might be used to.

The suits in the Creep's Cove deck are swords, guts, skulls, and bugs, but you can play with your plain ol' diamonds, clubs, hearts, and spades. In fact, it's pretty similar to the human game known as Go Fish!

HOW TO PLAY THE GAME:

Deal out seven cards to each player, and put the rest of the deck in the center of the altar/floor/table you're sitting around.

   The player with the sharpest teeth goes first by asking another player if they have any of a certain number or face card.* For example, "Theffanie, do you have any nines?"

   If Theffanie has any nines, they must surrender them to the player who asked and do one of the following (player's choice):

---

*NOTE: A PLAYER CAN ONLY ASK FOR CARDS THEY CURRENTLY HAVE AT LEAST ONE OF.

- Roar.
- Yell something to the effect of "THIS IS THE WORST DAY OF MY LIFE!"
- Sigh for at least five seconds.
- Fake cry.
- Boo at someone or something.

Then the player who asked gets to go again.

If Theffanie does *not* have any nines, Theffanie must yell, **"HOW DARE YOU ASK ME THAT?!"** Then the player who asked Theffanie for nines has to draw a card from the pile, and it's the next player's turn. Play proceeds clockwise around the circle. (Unless you're playing in the netherverse. Then, it's counterclockwise.)

At any point, when a player has four of a kind (example: four nines), that player should place all four cards faceup in front of them.

DECEIT:

Once per game, each player is allowed to "cheat" by pretending they do not have a card or cards being asked for. For example, if Theffanie is asked for nines, and she does have them but would like to hold on to them (and then immediately ask for nines on her turn), she can lie. Just once.

If you suspect a player of deceit, ask, "Do you speak the truth?!" If that player was lying, they must admit it and hand over the cards that were asked for. If the player was *not* being deceitful, the response is "How **VERY DARE** you ask me that?!" The player who so rudely accused their dear friend of deceit loses a turn.

Please be honest about your cheating.

WINNING:

The game ends when any one player has discarded all their cards in sets of four. Then every player counts their sets, and the player with the most sets wins.

To stay humble, the winner must ask the other players if they need any drink or snack refills.

How to Draw Lizzie

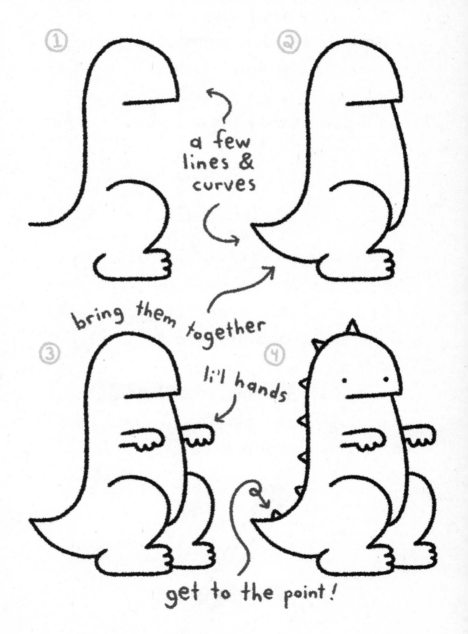

① ②

a few
lines &
curves

bring them together

③ ④

li'l hands

get to the point!

How to Draw Griff

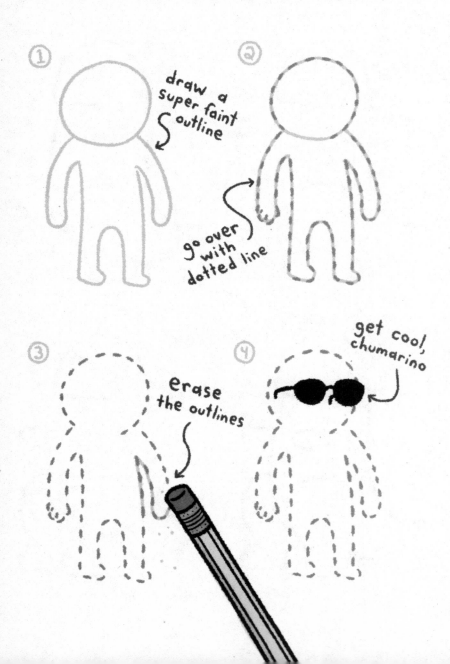

How to Draw Bobby

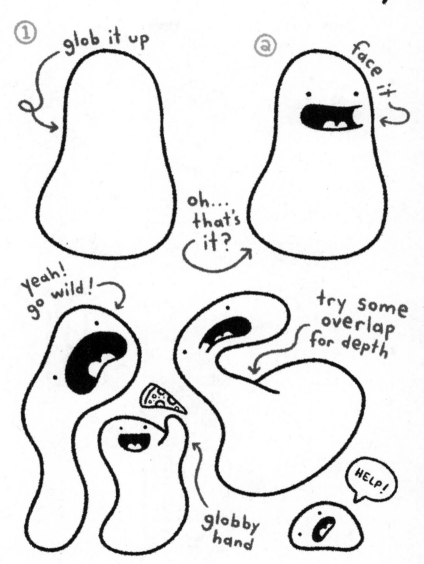

How to Draw Frankie

① safety goggles first

② hair & head curves

③ HI!

④ zigzag lab coat bits

⑤ Whoosh!

⑥ final touches and fills

BIO ALERT!

TRAVIS NICHOLS is the author and illustrator of a tidy heap of award-winning books and comics for kids and post-kids. When he's not writing and drawing, he's collecting and/or abandoning hobbies and representing Earth as an Adjunct Consulate in the Intergalactic Consortium. He lives in Brooklyn, New York, with some of his favorite creatures. You can find him puttering around in the garden.

IAMTRAVISNICHOLS.COM

 **@TRAVISNICHOLS**

@IAMTRAVISNICHOLS